ICE AGE™
DAWN OF THE DINOSAURS

SID-NAPPED

HarperCollins®, ✦®, and HarperEntertainment™
are trademarks of HarperCollins Publishers.

Ice Age: Dawn of the Dinosaurs: Sid-napped!
Ice Age Dawn of the Dinosaurs ™ & © 2009 Twentieth Century Fox Film Corporation.
All Rights Reserved. Printed in the United States of America.
No part of this book may be used or reproduced in any manner whatsoever without written permission except in the case
of brief quotations embodied in critical articles and reviews. For information address HarperCollins Children's Books,
a division of HarperCollins Publishers, 10 East 53rd Street, New York, NY 10022.
www.harpercollinschildrens.com

Library of Congress catalog card number: 2008942548
ISBN 978-0-06-168976-5

Typography by Joe Merkel
09 10 11 12 13 UG 10 9 8 7 6 5 4 3 2 1
❖
First Edition

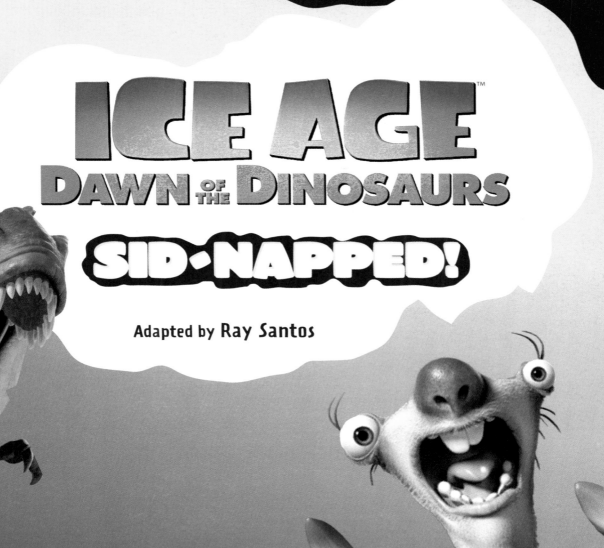

ICE AGE™
DAWN OF THE DINOSAURS
SID·NAPPED!

Adapted by Ray Santos

HARPER
ENTERTAINMENT
An Imprint of HarperCollinsPublishers

Two woolly mammoths named Manny and Ellie watched their friend Sid
slide around on the icy tundra. The sloth was juggling three giant eggs.
"Whatever you're doing is a bad idea," Manny said, as he shook his head.

"These eggs were under the ice all alone! Now they're my kids!" said Sid. "Someone's probably worried sick looking for them," Ellie added. "Mother birds fly away from their nests for hours. It doesn't mean they're not coming back." The mammoths wanted Sid to put the eggs back where he found them.

But on the way to return the eggs, Sid looked down at them and his heart melted. He wanted to keep the eggs and raise them. When it started to rain, he put the eggs under a rocky ledge to keep them dry. The sloth nestled next to his new family and fell asleep.

The next morning he woke up to the sound of
three baby dinosaurs calling out, "Momma! Momma!"
Sid was so happy!

Sid was playing with the little dinos when a giant Tyrannosaurus rex stomped up behind him and let out a big *ROOOAAAR!* It was Momma dinosaur!

"These are my kids," yelled Sid. "You're going to have to go through me to get them!"

But Momma wasn't scared of anything! She just reached down, snatched her three babies . . . and took Sid along for the ride! They all disappeared into a hole in the ground.

Manny, Ellie, and the two tiny possums, Eddie and Crash, saw the T. rex carry off their buddy. They looked down into the hole.

"Sid must be down there," Manny said.

The whole gang climbed down into an underground cavern. They were surprised to find Diego the saber-toothed tiger already down there. He was looking for Sid, too.

Then they heard a wild yell and looked up to
see a weasel with an eye patch swinging on a
vine. The weasel tossed several fruit bombs
at the ground to create a smoke screen in
front of the dinosaurs. "Fire in the hole!"
the weasel yelled as he leaped
to the ground.

"I'm Buck," the weasel said. "Follow me!" Hiding in the smoke, the gang ran away into the jungle with their new friend.

"So, how'd you guys get down here?" Buck asked once they reached a campsite.

"Our friend Sid was taken by a dinosaur," Ellie replied.

"A rescue mission!" Buck shouted.

Buck was willing to help them find Sid. "All right," Buck said. "I got rules. Rule number one: Always listen to Buck. Rule number two: Always stay in the middle of the trail."

The weasel's speech was interrupted by a loud *ROAAAR* in the distance followed by a familiar scream: "AAAAAAAAAAAAAAAAAH!!"
"Sid!" they all cried. They knew that their friend was in trouble.

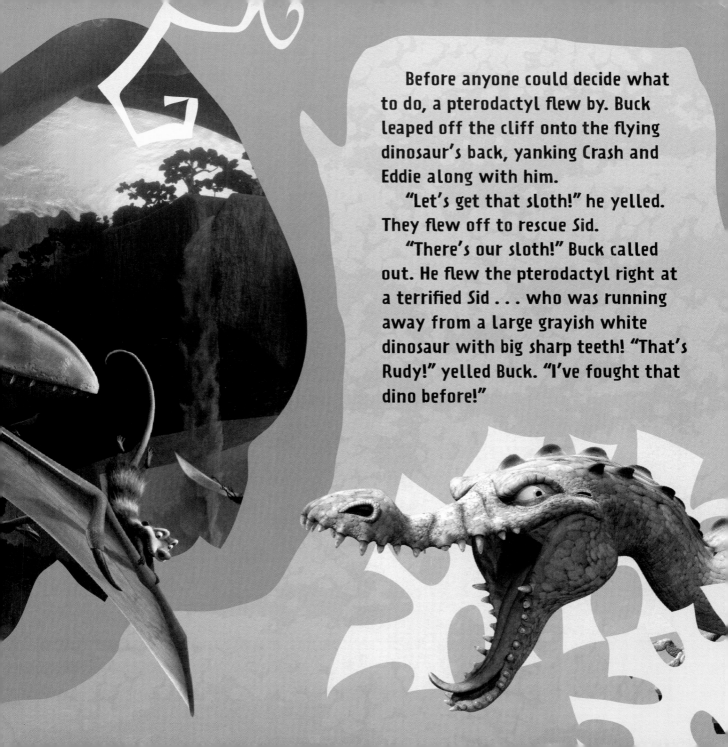

Before anyone could decide what to do, a pterodactyl flew by. Buck leaped off the cliff onto the flying dinosaur's back, yanking Crash and Eddie along with him.

"Let's get that sloth!" he yelled. They flew off to rescue Sid.

"There's our sloth!" Buck called out. He flew the pterodactyl right at a terrified Sid . . . who was running away from a large grayish white dinosaur with big sharp teeth! "That's Rudy!" yelled Buck. "I've fought that dino before!"

Sid screamed when the pterodactyl grabbed him in its talons. He didn't know that it was his friends coming to save him!

They landed safely in front of the mammoths and Diego.

"Sid, it's Crash and Eddie," the two possums said. "We're all here looking for you."

"The whole gang? For me?" Sid replied. He couldn't believe that his friends had come to find him.

Manny smiled as Sid wrapped himself around his friend's long trunk. The sloth was happy to see his friends again.

"You're pretty lucky to be part of this family," said Buck. After a big group hug, the gang turned to head back home to the tundra together.